Shattered Star

CHARNAN SIMON

SURVIVING SOUTHSIDE

Shattered Star

Charnan Simon

darbycreek

MINNEAPOLIS

Darby Creek
A division of Lerner Publishing Group, Inc.
241 First Avenue North
Minneapolis, MN 55401 U.S.A.

Website address: www.lernerbooks.com

The images in this book are used with the permission of:
© Jason Stitt/Shutterstock Images, (main image)
front cover; © iStockphoto.com/Jill Fromer, (banner
background) front cover and throughout interior;
© iStockphoto.com/Naphtalina, (brick wall background)
front and back cover and throughout interior.

Library of Congress Cataloging-in-Publication Data

Simon, Charnan.
    Shattered star / Charnan Simon.
      p. cm. — (Surviving Southside)
    ISBN 978-0-7613-6154-1 (lib. bdg. : alk. paper)
    [1. Singing—Fiction. 2. High schools—Fiction.
  3. Schools—Fiction. 4. Hispanic Americans—Fiction.]
  I. Title.
PZ7.S6035Sf 2011
[Fic]—dc22   2010023655

Manufactured in the United States of America
1 – BP – 12/31/10

For my expert advisers,
Hawa, Liz, Taylor,
and Bailey
—C.S.

CHAPTER 1

I nailed my solo.

I knew it even before the last note died and the applause started. "Defying Gravity" from *Wicked* has always been one of my favorite songs. Now I was singing it solo for our glee club's spring concert. I had been practicing for weeks. Tonight, I had put my whole heart and soul into that song. With the audience whistling and clapping, nothing could bring me down.

Ms. Cao, our director, waved at me to take another bow. Then I stepped back to my spot on the risers. The curtain came down. When the applause didn't stop, the curtain rose again. This time, the whole glee club bowed. Twice more the curtain dropped and rose. Three curtain calls! It was our best concert ever.

We were all buzzing when the curtain finally stayed down and the house lights came up. Estela ran over from the alto section. She threw her arms around me.

"Amazing!" she shrieked. "You were awesome! You rule!" Estela's a good best friend. She doesn't hold back when it comes to anything.

Even Julia Posada had something nice to say. "Good job, Cassie."

I knew Julia wanted to sing the solo. "Thanks," I said. I was feeling generous. "You would have sung it well, too."

"I know," Julia said. "Just wait till sectionals!"

What a snob! I started to say something

not quite so generous, but then Domingo Mendes came over. Domingo swept me up into a hug, and thoughts of Julia faded. "You did good, neighbor!" he said. "You might even say . . . wicked good!"

I groaned at Domingo's bad pun. Then I blushed. Domingo and I have been next-door neighbors forever. Lately, though, I've been wondering if we might be more than neighbors. Did Domingo's hug mean he felt the same way?

Estela raised her eyebrows at me. "Come along, children," she said. "Let's find the families. Then I need food! I was too excited to eat dinner."

The auditorium lobby was crowded. So many people stopped to congratulate me that I felt like a star. When I finally found Mom, she was beaming.

"Cassie, you were wonderful!" She gave me a huge hug. "I sent your dad a video from my phone. He said that next time I have to stay home with Jake and Ray. He wants his turn to see you sing in person!"

I laughed, but I felt kind of bad, too. My little brothers can't stay up late enough for glee club concerts. Tonight, Dad lost the coin toss. (He claimed Mom had rigged it.) He had to stay home to put them to bed.

Mom gave me another quick hug. "I have to run, sweetie," she said. "Mrs. McVey will be waiting for me, and you know how she worries. Do you have a ride home?"

Mom is a home-health aide. Mrs. McVey is one of her favorite clients. Mrs. McVey is over ninety years old. She still lives in her own house. She just needs Mom to help her get ready for bed at night.

Just then Estela came up. Domingo was right behind her. "Hi, Mrs. Pratt," Estela said. "Don't worry about Cassie. Domingo's giving us a ride home. Right, Domingo?"

"Sure," he said. "Okay if we stop for something to eat on the way home?"

Mom likes Domingo. "Of course," she said, smiling. "Just not too late. It's still a school night!"

I shook my head while Mom hurried off

through the crowd. You'd think I was still in middle school, the way Mom talks, instead of a junior who just sang the star solo!

chApTER 2

The Daily Grind was crowded. Everyone must have been hungry after the concert. Domingo found a table while Estela and I went up to the counter.

"That boy likes you," Estela said as we waited in line.

I turned red and started to protest. What was with my face anyhow? Nobody blushes anymore!

Luckily, it was our turn to order, so I didn't

have to answer. Todd, the guy behind the counter, is a senior at Southside. "I hear you kicked butt tonight, Cassie!" he said. "Too bad I had to work and miss the concert."

I didn't even know Todd knew my name! I could get used to being a star.

Estela ordered a muffin and two mochas with whipped cream, for her and Domingo. "Make one a grande," she said. "I'm thirsty after all that singing." She fumbled in her purse. "I know I have a ten in here somewhere."

I knew I didn't have a ten. "Small coffee, please," I told Todd. "Lots of room for cream."

Estela isn't rich or anything. She babysits for her spending money. But Estela's parents are both teachers. They have good, steady jobs. They pay for Estela's clothes and school supplies.

My dad's job at the Best Foods warehouse was cut to part-time this winter. Mom picked up more clients, but she can't work 24-7. And a home-health aide's salary doesn't go far. I've added more hours to my job at Taco Shack.

I'm pretty careful about where I spend my money. I can always eat a sandwich when I get home.

We worked our way over to the table. Lots of kids stopped to tell me how well I sang.

"Our little girl's famous," Estela said as she slid into her chair. "I guess we're lucky she'll still sit with us!"

Domingo laughed. "You really were great, Cassie," he said. "I mean, I've always known you could sing. But tonight was something else! You sounded like a pro!"

Estela nearly choked on her mocha.

"Thanks for the vote of confidence," I said. I was laughing, but her reaction stung a bit.

Estela coughed and spluttered. "That isn't what I meant, Cassie," she said. She dug through her purse again. "I knew I was forgetting something! Here!" She shoved a crumpled flyer over the table to me.

I smoothed out the flyer. "*America's Next Star*: Your Turn in the Spotlight!" I read out loud. "What's this, Estela?"

"It's your chance to make it big! I got it off the bulletin board at the bowling alley. Look! *America's Next Star* is auditioning right here in Houston! You should try out!"

Now I really was laughing. "Oh, right! Me on *America's Next Star*—like that's going to happen!"

Domingo leaned over to read the flyer. "No, really, Cassie. I think Estela's right. You should totally do this!"

I have the best friends in the world. "You two are great," I said. "But I don't think *America's Next Star* is for kids like me. It's for kids who have singing lessons and acting coaches and real costumes and, well, everything I don't have."

Estela tossed her head. "They don't have your voice," she insisted. "And they don't have your stage presence. You should have seen yourself tonight. You were *on*!"

That made me feel really good. "Thanks," I said. "But are you guys almost ready to go home? I still have all my math homework."

Estela made a face. "You're so boring, girl," she said. "I want to make you a star, and all you can think about is math!"

As we left, I slipped the *America's Next Star* flyer into my bag. I don't think anyone saw me.

Later, alone in my bedroom, I read the flyer carefully. Tryouts were next Thursday and were for kids eighteen and under. I just needed to show up at the theater with an audition song. The ten winners won two-thousand-dollar college scholarships and a trip to Los Angeles. In L.A., singers from all over the country would compete against each other. The top five would win five thousand dollar scholarships and a chance to sing live on *America's Next Star.* Then the audience would vote. The singer they liked best would win ten thousand dollars. He or she would also get a chance to record with a real music studio!

I turned out the light and lay in bed thinking. *I love glee club. I want to go to college and study music. Someday, I want to be a glee club director like Ms. Cao. But Mom and Dad*

can't afford college. Even a two-thousand-dollar
scholarship would be huge. A chance to record with
a real music studio would be even better. Maybe
I really am that good. Maybe I'm better than
Southside glee club. Maybe I could be a star!

Who am I kidding? I thought as I fell asleep.
I could never win.

But then I realized, until I tried, I'd never
know—just like a line from my solo. I made
up my mind. I wouldn't tell anyone, not even
Estela, in case I bombed. But next Thursday I,
Cassie Pratt, was trying out for *America's Next
Star!*

ChApTeR 3

The day of the *America's Next Star* tryouts came fast. I set my alarm a half hour early. I wanted plenty of time to get ready.

I took an extra-long shower. I spent a lot of time on my hair and makeup. Then I looked at my clothes. It seemed strange not to call Estela for advice. Estela's more fashionable than I am. She's got a great eye. She can always make an outfit really stand out. Still, I thought she would like my choices. I put on my favorite short jean skirt and a bright purple scoop-neck tank. Then I added my long black button-up tunic. But what about shoes? Heels? Too dressy. Flats? Too boring. In the end, I decided my wedge sandals worked best.

Finally, I put on the chunky crystal necklace Estela had given me for my birthday. I could hear her voice as I fastened the clasp. "Don't be afraid of big jewelry! Every outfit needs a piece of interest. A headband's good. But with a scoop neck, the right necklace is even better!"

Getting dressed turned out to be the easy part. Dad dropped me off at school on his way to work. I waited outside until he drove away. I felt bad not telling Mom and Dad what I was up to, but they're such sticklers about not skipping school. Skipping for a long shot, like trying out for *America's Next Star*—I just didn't think that they'd buy it. They're proud of my singing and all, but they don't really see it as a realistic way to earn a living. If I won the audition, it would be a great surprise—and maybe they'd change their minds.

I looked around to make sure I didn't see any of my friends. Usually I meet Estela at our lockers. We have first-period math together. But today I wasn't going to math. I wasn't going to any classes. I was even planning on skipping after-school glee club rehearsal. I knew Ms. Cao wouldn't like that at all. Sectionals were coming up in a few weeks, and we all needed to be preparing like crazy. Especially me, since I wanted to sing a solo. Still, missing one rehearsal couldn't hurt too much. And imagine Ms. Cao's face when I told her I had won a trip to L.A. with *America's Next Star*!

I hurried down the block to the nearest bus stop. I had never taken the bus downtown before. But I had looked up the schedule online last night. It didn't look hard. I thought I should have to change buses only once. And the map showed that the bus station wasn't *that* far from the theater where the auditions were being held. I could walk the rest of the way—even in sandals.

Three hours and three buses later I was tired, sweaty, and kicking myself. I must not have read the schedule right. The first bus I took was okay. It got me away from Southside High and headed toward downtown. I got off at the stop I had written down. But then I had to wait and wait for the second bus. When it finally came, it must have been the wrong one. Instead of going downtown, it headed toward the airport! I got off and tried a third bus. But that one was wrong, too. Finally, I told the bus driver that I was lost. Luckily, she was nice. She told me the buses I needed and made sure that I wrote down the right numbers and the right stops.

By the time I got to the theater, I felt like crying. The crowds were huge! Police officers were there to keep everyone in order.

"Excuse me," I asked a guy holding a clipboard. "Do I need to sign up or anything?"

"Get a number," he said. He didn't even

look at me. "At the main door. Then get in line with everyone else."

I had to push just to reach the door. "You're pretty late," said the woman handing out numbers. "People have been lined up for hours."

I started to explain about the buses and everything.

"Just take your number," she said, sounding bored.

I looked at the card the woman handed me. I was number 847. "Excuse me," I said again. "Does this mean there are 846 people ahead of me?"

The woman looked even more bored. "It does," she said. "Some of them are already in the theater. The rest are lined up outside. So get in line. You have a long wait in front of you."

Now I really felt like crying, and I felt like a fool. This was what I had skipped school for . . . to be number 847? I slowly walked back through the crowd. I was hot and tired and thirsty. I needed to use the bathroom.

My tunic was wrinkled from all the bus rides. I had a blister on my baby toe from all the walking in uncomfortable sandals. I didn't even know where the end of the line was!

I didn't feel quite like a star anymore.

CHAPTER 4

I had to ask three people before I found the end of the line. It snaked around the parking lot in an endless loop. I took my place and got ready to wait.

Luckily, the girl in front of me was friendly. "Hi," she said. "I'm Olivia. I'm glad somebody's even later than me." Then she made an awkward face. "Sorry . . . that sounded mean."

"That's okay," I said. "Nobody wants to be

last." I dug around in my purse for my brush. "I could sure use a mirror and a sink."

Olivia nodded. "Across the street," she said. "There's a coffee shop with a bathroom. But you have to buy something. I'll save your place if you want."

"Thanks," I said. "That would be so, so great!"

I hurried across the street to the coffee shop. I was absolutely starving, so I splurged and got a muffin with my small iced coffee. Then I found the bathroom. Ten minutes later I had my face washed and my hair brushed. I fixed my makeup. The world always looks better with fresh mascara and a new coat of lip gloss.

Back in line, I started talking to Olivia. She turned out to be a senior at West High. "I had the lead in our school musical last year," she said. "I want to move to L.A. when I graduate . . . or maybe New York. Although it's totally my dream to live in Paris. If I don't make it as a singer or an actor, maybe I'll model."

Olivia looked like a model. She was tall and dark, with huge eyes.

"Have you ever been to one of these tryouts before?" I asked.

"Nope," she shook her head. "But I've heard they're pretty tough. You go inside in groups, and you only get to sing a little bit. You don't sing your whole song. They just cut you off! Otherwise they'd never make it through everyone."

This was news to me. "So how do they pick?" I asked. "If you don't even get to finish your song?"

Olivia shrugged. "You just have to stand out in some way. Either you look really good or you sound really good. Maybe both if you're really talented."

Well, Olivia certainly looked good. "What's your song?" I asked.

"'Don't Stop Believin'" she said. "It's a pretty good song for my voice. I thought for a while about 'Defying Gravity,' but then I figured half the girls here will be singing that one."

I felt myself turning red.

Olivia laughed. "See!" she said. "That's your song, isn't it?"

When I nodded, Olivia patted my arm. "Don't worry," she said. "I'm just being mean again. The other half of the girls will probably be singing my song!"

She was probably right. Both our songs were really popular.

I looked around at the crowd. Everyone was dressed up and excited. Some kids had guitars. One girl carried a sign that read "Kiss Me, It's My Birthday!" A guy just ahead of us was wearing an all-white tuxedo with a white cowboy hat. Another guy wore a sleeveless black T-shirt that showed off all his tattoos. Every now and then, someone sang a few notes of a song. Other kids joined in or started their own songs.

"This is a total zoo," Olivia said.

"For real," I replied. I tried to muffle my laugh after Olivia started imitating the tattoo guy.

It was a good thing there was so much to watch. The line barely moved. Every so often, one group came out of the theater and another group went in. Otherwise, we stood still. More people came to stand behind me. Olivia and I held each other's places in line to take bathroom breaks.

I didn't realize how much time had gone by until my cell rang. It was Roz, my manager at Taco Shack. "Cassie!" Roz sounded frazzled. "Where are you? Your shift started fifteen minutes ago!"

Impossible! I checked the time on my cell. When did it get to be four fifteen? "Roz, I'm really sorry," I stammered. "I . . . I have an emergency. Can Kelsey or Taylor cover for me?"

"Kelsey's already gone," Roz said. "I had to let her leave ten minutes ago. And Taylor has a dentist appointment. What's your emergency? Are you sick?"

"Not exactly—," I started to say, but Roz cut me off.

"Because if you aren't bleeding or throwing up, you had better get here quick. I can cover for you till five, but that's it. You were late twice last week because of glee club. Then there was your concert. You either show up to your shifts on time or you don't work. You're going to have to choose! Lots of other kids want this job if you don't!"

chAptER 5

"Problems?" Olivia asked as I put away my cell.

"That was my boss," I said gloomily. "I'm late for work. This is taking so long!"

A man with a clipboard was standing nearby. "Hi," he said. "I couldn't help overhearing. Got a problem sticking around for this?"

"Yes," I said. "Is there any way I can do my audition soon? I have to get to work!"

He shook his head. "I doubt it," he said. "But I'm not with *America's Next Star.* The way those clowns run these auditions is awful. Making kids wait around all day like this . . . and for what? So you can sing for fifteen seconds and then get cut? Cattle calls like this ought to be against the law!"

He shook his head again. Then he smiled at me. "Sorry to sound off," he said. "My name's Harold King. I'm a talent scout, out from L.A. It makes me crazy to see you kids treated this way."

"You're a talent scout," I said, "from L.A.?" I looked at Mr. King more closely. He was maybe my dad's age, but he dressed way different. His black shirt was open at the collar, with the sleeves rolled up. I could tell his jeans were a designer brand. He had dark blue eyes with nice crinkle lines in a really tanned face. Even though it was so hot, he looked cool, somehow.

Mr. King handed me a business card and a flyer. "Harold King, STAR 1," I read. "The hunt is on for new talent! STAR 1 is one of the largest talent companies in the country. With offices in major cities, we have everything you need to launch your career."

"If you aren't with *America's Next Star*, why are you here?" asked Olivia. She sounded like she didn't believe him.

Mr. King nodded. "Good question. I travel all over the country. It's my business to go to as many of these auditions as I possibly can. Talented kids in every city show up. It's a great place to scout." He hesitated. "I don't want to lie to you girls. I'm sure everyone here is talented. But I'm only interested in a specific look. I won't waste my time—or yours—if I don't think you have it."

Olivia still looked skeptical.

Mr. King looked directly at me. "And you, young lady, have a look my agency could really use!"

"I do?"

"Absolutely! That gorgeous long hair and those great eyes! Look . . . you can stay here if you want. But it's getting late. And you're still far back in line. You might have to come back tomorrow or even the next day. Instead, why not let me do a screen test tomorrow afternoon? We'll make a personal video, and I'll listen to your range. It won't take more than an hour or so. But that's really just a formality. I know my L.A. office is going to want to see you in person. I'd bet on it. We'll get some travel vouchers and fly you out. What do you think?"

What did I think? I thought it sounded a lot better than standing around in this line! But was Mr. King for real?

I looked at Olivia. "What should I do?"

Olivia shrugged. "I'm staying here," she said. She sounded miffed that Mr. King wasn't interested in her. "But he's right that we'll probably have to come back tomorrow. I heard they close up by five."

Mr. King smiled at me encouragingly. "I can give you a ride to work if you want," he said. "No point in making your boss mad. We can set up an appointment for tomorrow on the way."

I hesitated. How many times had I heard

never accept a ride from strangers? But that was when I was a kid. And Mr. King wasn't really a stranger—I had his business card right in my hand. Anyhow, professional talent scouts weren't kidnappers!

My cell phone rang—Roz again. "I don't know . . ."

Mr. King nodded. "I understand. Take all the time you need," he said. "My phone number's on my card. I'll be in town through the weekend if you want to set up an appointment. And good luck with your audition here!" He started to move away through the crowd.

Then, just like that, I made up my mind. I couldn't miss another day of school to come back here tomorrow. And I definitely couldn't risk losing my job at Taco Shack. This was the only way.

I felt nervous and excited as I snapped open my phone.

"Hi, Roz," I said. "I'm really sorry to be late. But I'm on my way!" I put away my phone. I told Olivia good-bye and good luck.

Then I ran to catch up with Mr. King. "I'll take that ride, if you're still offering. It's the Taco Shack on Taft."

"Not a problem," he said warmly. "And please, call me Hal."

CHAPTER 6

Mr. King—Hal—got me to work. He was really nice on the drive. He asked me about school and glee club and my family. He was so easy to talk to that I felt comfortable right away.

"Screen test tomorrow!" he called out when I got out of his car at Taco Shack. "Don't forget!"

"Not a chance!" I might be a little nervous about the screen test, but I was *not* worried about forgetting something that could change my whole life!

I had to close at Taco Shack. That meant I didn't get home until late. Mom was at Mrs. McVey's for the night. Dad was already asleep and snoring.

I stuck my head in his room. "I'm home," I whispered. It's the house rule. Since I turned seventeen, I don't really have a curfew. But I have to let Mom or Dad know when I come in at night.

"Hmmm-mmmm," Dad sort of growled, half asleep.

I wanted to go to sleep too. But first I had to call Estela. I had been texting her with excuses all day.

"About time!" Estela said when she answered. "How's Jakey?"

For a second, I blanked. Then I remembered my story. I had told Estela I wasn't in school because Jake was sick and both my parents had to work. I said they couldn't find a babysitter, so I had to stay home and watch him.

"He's a lot better," I said uncomfortably. It felt wrong to be lying to Estela, especially about my little brother. "He'll be back in school tomorrow."

"Good," said Estela. "I almost stopped by to see you after school. But glee club ran longer than usual. We're starting solo auditions for sectionals tomorrow. And get this: Julia's telling everyone she's going to beat you out!"

For a minute I panicked. What if Estela had stopped by my house this afternoon? This lying business was harder than it seemed.

But I couldn't worry about that now. Glee club sectional tryouts were tomorrow! Right when I'd be meeting with Hal!

"Ms. Cao is doing the guys' solos first," Estela went on. "I think Domingo's going to try out. It would be so cool if you both got solos!"

Whew! I was safe, at least for now. Maybe this would even work out in my favor. Ms. Cao might not mind if I skipped the boys' solos tomorrow.

Estela and I talked a little more. She gave me my assignments for math and English.

I spent nearly two hours plowing through homework. It was after one A.M. when I finally climbed into bed and turned out the lights.

Then I got up and turned them back on. I had to write an excuse for missing school. I knew other kids forged notes from their parents all the time. But I never had. Lying to Estela felt strange, but faking my mom's handwriting felt even stranger.

What if I just told my parents where I had been and what I had done today? They'd be mad about skipping school. But wouldn't they be excited about my audition with Hal?

Maybe . . . maybe not. At the very least, they'd probably insist on coming to the screen test with me. And I wanted this to be my secret, my surprise.

I signed my mom's signature. I stuck the note in my backpack. There would be plenty of time to tell everyone about Hal when I was on my way to L.A.

I fell asleep dreaming about my first album. "That gorgeous hair and great eyes." That's what Hal had said about me. It sounded like a line from a song.

CHAPTER 7

I didn't want to wake up when my alarm went off. But then I remembered my screen test with Hal. I jumped out of bed. I threw open my closet door.

What to wear? Hal said he was shooting a video. I needed to look really good. I must have tried on half my clothes before I finally picked an outfit. I decided on my favorite skinny jeans, my black baby-doll top, and shiny gold flats. I added big gold hoop earrings and gold chains.

"You look nice this morning," Mom said when I walked into the kitchen. She looked sleepy. It must have been a long night at Mrs. McVey's. Mom held back a yawn between sentences. "Something special at school today?"

"Sectional solo tryouts in glee club," I said. I was getting good at lying, fast.

"Break a leg!" Dad said as he helped Ray pour milk on his cereal. My stomach growled a bit, but I felt too nervous to eat.

"Why do you want Cassie to break her leg?" asked Jake. He looked worried. "Won't it hurt?"

"It's just a saying," I assured him. "It's how you say *good luck* in showbiz."

Ray and Jake thought this was hilarious. "Break your leg!" they crowed as I grabbed a banana and headed for the door. "Break both your legs!"

Domingo always gives me a ride to school on Fridays. "I hear you're trying out for a sectionals solo," I said as I slid into his car.

"Yeah," he said. "Got my fingers crossed." He looked at me sideways. "Missed you in school yesterday. Estela said you had to stay home with Jake . . ."

I nodded, looking out the window. I couldn't quite meet his eyes.

Domingo was quiet for a minute. "Funny," he said. "I could have sworn I saw Jake and Ray playing in the yard yesterday. Your dad was calling them in for dinner when I got home from glee club."

What could I say? I was lying, and Domingo knew it.

"Are you stalking me or something?" I forced a laugh so Domingo would know I was just kidding around.

We spent the rest of the ride in an awkward silence. A couple of times I opened my mouth to tell him about *America's Next Star* and Hal. Then I snapped it shut again. It would make a much better story when I had a signed contract from Hal's talent agency in my hand!

The morning crawled past. I couldn't stop thinking about my appointment with Hal. He was picking me up right after school.

At lunch, Estela was too mad about yearbooks to notice how quiet I was. "They were supposed to come out today," she complained. "I brought my sixty dollars and everything. But now they've been delayed till Monday. People aren't going to be excited about signing them then. Who passes out yearbooks on a Monday? It's whack. Everybody has their money today!"

She was right. I had my sixty bucks with me too. "I raided my Taco Shack tip jar," I said. "There's still over two hundred dollars. I really need to put it in the bank before I spend it all."

"Or how about this instead?" Estela suggested. "This weekend is the sidewalk sale at the mall. It's perfect. I need sandals, and you need jeans. Let's check it out. We could go today, right after glee club. I bet Domingo would give us a ride. I'll even offer to pay for gas."

"I can't—," I started to say. But my cell phone rang. It was Hal.

"Hi, Cassie," he said. "I'm just making sure we're still on for this afternoon. I'm picking you up at three forty-five across the street from the school parking lot, right?"

"Sure," I said. "See you then." I hung up in sort of a hurry. I didn't want to talk to Hal in front of Estela.

"Who was that?" she asked.

"Um . . . just my dad," I said. "That's what I was going to tell you. I can't go to the mall today. I have to go right home."

"How come?" Estela persisted. "Is Jake still sick?"

"No," I said, trying to think of an excuse. "Jake's fine."

"Then why?" Estela asked impatiently. "And what about glee club? You're going to miss it again? Ms. Cao is going to be peeved, girl."

I was tired of thinking up lies. "Yes," I snapped. "I'm going to miss glee club again! It's family stuff. Ms. Cao will just have to understand!"

But Ms. Cao didn't understand. After lunch, I stopped by the music room to plead my case. Somehow, I think she knew what I was going to say before I even started.

"Um. Ms. Cao, I'm sorry," I began, "but I can't stay after for glee club today. I've got a conflict."

Mrs. Cao frowned. "This will be the second day in a row that you've missed, Cassie," she said. "Sectionals are next month. We have a lot of rehearsing to do. And I thought you wanted to try out for a solo."

"I do!" I said. "But aren't you auditioning the boys today? It isn't like I'd really be missing anything."

Ms. Cao shook her head. "You know the drill, Cassie. I like everyone to support our soloists. We're all in this together. And the auditions won't take all afternoon. We'll still practice for at least half an hour, and I want everyone there for that too. Is it something going on at home? Do you want me to talk to your parents?"

Why was everyone making this so hard? "No!" I said. "I need to take care of my little brother this afternoon. He's sick, and both my parents have to work. I'm really sorry, but I just can't stay today!"

I left the music room in a hurry. Estela watched me go. Domingo was standing by the window. I couldn't be sure, but I thought he saw me get into Hal's waiting car.

CHAPTER 8

I was still upset when I got in Hal's car. But he made me feel better right away.

"Hi, Cassie," he said cheerfully. "It's great to see you again! Here . . . I picked up some donuts at Shipley's. I figured you might be hungry after school. Help yourself!"

I love Shipley's donuts. And Hal had my favorite: chocolate twists. My mood definitely improved as I munched.

"I've been thinking about you all day," Hal

went on. "I called our L.A. office right after I dropped you off yesterday. Usually, I wait until I do a demo video. I like to see how singers look on camera. But I know the camera's going to love you."

He laughed and shook his head. "And to think I almost left before I saw you yesterday! I was on my way to my car. I had been at those auditions all day. I hadn't seen anyone with the right look. Then you jumped out at me and I knew—bingo! My lucky day!"

More like my lucky day, I thought.

"Thanks for the ride," I said, a little shy. "I could have taken the bus. But it would have taken a lot longer."

"Not a problem!" Hal said comfortably. "I don't usually drive clients. At least not until we have a contract. But like I say . . . you're special. I don't want to waste any time signing you up!"

As he was talking, Hal pulled into the valet parking at the Dahlia Hotel.

I got a little nervous. "I thought we were going to your office," I blurted.

Hal patted my knee. "This *is* my office," he said reassuringly. "I travel all over the country, remember?" He gave little laugh. "The agency leases hotel suites for me to use. This way, I have Internet and room service and comfortable furniture. It's more efficient and economical than setting up a temporary office."

He looked at me keenly, then paused. "If you'd rather, Cassie, we can shoot the video in the lobby. It won't be quite as good, because of all the background noises. But you're calling the shots here."

Hal's blue eyes were dark with concern. I felt stupid for being nervous. I must have sounded like such a dumb kid. "Oh no," I said. "The suite is fine."

The suite *was* fine. In fact, it was fantastic. Hal gave me a sparkling water from the little bar. He poured it in a tall glass with lots of ice and a wedge of lime. "Next time, you can bring your swimsuit," he said. "There's a pool on the roof. You can go up and swim while I do paperwork. I don't swim. But it'd be a

shame not to get any use out of the pool . . .
great views, too."

While Hal set up the video camera, I
looked around. One whole wall was windows.
The other walls were draped with heavy
black fabric. Glossy pictures were pinned up
everywhere: pictures of glamorous people—
people who looked like stars. "Are these your
clients?" I asked shyly.

"Yep," Hal said. "You can see why I
thought you'd fit right in. Same look, only
better!"

Then Hal turned businesslike. "Stand
away from the window," he directed. "I don't
want you backlit for this."

Then I started singing, and he started
taping. At first I was a little shaky.

"Relax!" he said encouragingly. "You're
doing just great!"

When we were done shooting, Hal opened
a file on the desk. "Okay," he said. "Now what
about a portfolio? Did you bring one with
you? We'll need some still shots as well as the
video."

Portfolio? What portfolio? My heart sank.

"I . . . I don't have a portfolio," I stammered. Was this going to keep me from going to L.A.?

Hal was quick to reassure me. "No worries," he said. "I prefer taking photos myself. But sometimes artists insist on using their own." He thumbed through an appointment book. "Can we schedule a photo shoot for Tuesday—same time, right after school? I'll pick you up."

"Sure," I said. Then I had a thought. "But . . . don't professional pictures cost a lot of money? I'm not sure I can afford them."

Hal nodded briskly. "The usual rate is $795." He must have noticed my shocked expression. He added quickly, "But don't worry about the price. Like I said, all this is just a formality. I know my agency will sign you up. What can you afford?"

"I have sixty dollars with me," I said slowly. I was thinking about my yearbook money. "And I can get maybe another two hundred. I don't think I can ask my parents for more."

"No, no," said Hal. "Don't worry about asking your parents. How about this: I'll take the sixty for a deposit today. You can bring the other two hundred on Tuesday. I'll cover the rest out of my own pocket. I have a special feeling about you, Cassie. I think you're going to be big, really big! I don't mind fronting you a few hundred dollars."

Hal was so nice! He gave me a receipt for my sixty dollars. Then he had me sign a release for the video. "It's for your own protection," he said. "You need someone to take care of you in this business."

When we finished, he took me up to the roof. The pool was amazing! It was all gleaming white tiles and cool turquoise water. Around the deck were comfy lounge chairs and big potted plants. The view stretched on forever.

"How about it, Cassie?" Hal asked. He stood close behind me. We looked out over the city together. His hands rested lightly on my shoulders.

"Can you get used to a life like this?" Hal asked softly. "Because this is what it will be when I make you a star!"

CHAPTER 9

All weekend I felt like I would burst with excitement. I was going to be a star! I kept reliving that moment on the rooftop of the Dahlia Hotel: the city spread out before me, Hal's hands on my shoulders, his voice in my ear, "Can you get used to a life like this?"

And then when he drove me home, the way he looked deep in my eyes. "You aren't just any client, Cassie," he said. "I mean it when I say you're special. You know that, don't you?"

I shivered just thinking about it.

Part of me really, really wanted to talk about Hal. This was the biggest thing that ever happened to me. But another part wanted to hug my secret tight. Hal said that he'd have my L.A. travel voucher on Tuesday. That's when I'd tell everyone. That's when I'd let my secret become real.

In the meantime, I had to deal with Estela. I called her first thing Saturday morning. I pretended nothing had happened.

"Hey," I said. "So . . . what about the sidewalk sale? Do you still want to look for sandals? I don't have to work until six."

There was a short silence on the other end of the line. "Are you sure you don't have any family stuff?" Estela asked, a bit coldly.

"Nope, not a thing," I answered breezily. "My dad says I can have the car. Should I pick you up?"

Estela can't stay mad. And she loves to shop. "Okay!" she said. "I just need to jump into the shower. Give me half an hour!"

It was a little tricky, going to a sale and not buying anything. Estela knew exactly how much tip money I had. But I needed to save it all for Hal's pictures.

"You're making me nuts!" Estela finally burst out. "You've tried on hundreds of pairs of jeans! Except for those awful ones at Bargain Bin, they all look great. Why won't you buy any?"

"I don't know," I said. "I'm just not in the mood. They make my butt look big."

Estela rolled her eyes. "You're crazy," she said. Then she bought herself two pairs of sandals. "Look at me! I'm buying double to make up for you!"

I wasn't feeling any less crazy by Monday. School had never gone so slowly. I wanted Tuesday afternoon to hurry up and get here!

I was still thinking about Hal when I walked into glee club. It took me a minute to figure out why everyone was so excited. Then it hit me. Today was sectional solo auditions! How could I have forgotten?

Estela hurried up to me. "Good luck, girlfriend!" she said. "Did you see the posting? Domingo won his solo spot. Now all you have to do is nail yours!"

My solo! I was planning to sing "You Belong with Me," but I had hardly practiced since the spring concert. I should have worked on my song instead of shopping this weekend.

"Julia's telling everyone that she's going to beat you," Estela went on. "I think she means more than just the solo. That girl has her eye on Domingo."

I looked over at Julia. Estela was right. Julia was leaning way too close to Domingo as they thumbed through the sheet music on the piano.

Estela gave me a quick, tight hug. "You can do this!"

I should have nailed this solo, too. But as it turned out . . . I didn't. I was too flustered. Thinking about Hal and L.A. wasn't helping my life at Southside. Nothing went right during my audition. I came in on the wrong beat. I flubbed the lyrics. I couldn't get the tempo right.

Estela looked stricken. Domingo looked concerned. Ms. Cao frowned.

It was a complete and total disaster.

Julia, on the other hand, was brilliant. She sang "Halo" as if the song had been written for her. She started out deep and sultry. Her voice grew stronger and richer with every note. By the end, she was soaring. The room erupted in an outburst of applause. Even *I* had to clap.

What would Hal think if he were here? Would he like Julia better than me? I pushed the thoughts aside.

Ms. Cao stopped me on my way out. "I'm surprised at you, Cassie," she said, "surprised and disappointed. This was an important solo for you. It could have helped you get that music scholarship you want."

What could I say? She was right. But I didn't need a music scholarship now. I was going to L.A.!

When I didn't answer, Ms. Cao went on. "I don't know what has gotten into you, Cassie. First you skip glee club. Then you throw away this audition. Just because I gave you the spring concert solo doesn't mean you can coast for the rest of the year."

When I still didn't say anything, Ms. Cao looked angry. "I'll give you one more chance, Cassie," she said sharply. "We all work together in glee club. You need to shape up! If you don't . . . don't count on going to sectionals."

CHAPTER 10

I was still steaming when I left school, thinking about what Ms. Cao had said. *How could she talk to me that way? I'm her best singer! Oh, sure, Julia did well today. But I've been Ms. Cao's favorite all year! How could she turn on me like this just because I messed up one day?*

I heard a car honk. Domingo pulled up next to me. "Hey," he called. "Where are you going? Aren't I giving you a ride to work?"

Work! I was blanking on everything these days! My Taco Shack shift started in fifteen minutes! "Thanks," I said as I got in the car. "I forgot you said you'd give me a ride."

"That's okay," Domingo said. "You've had a rough afternoon."

I knew he was talking about my solo audition. "More like a stupid afternoon," I said. "I don't know what happened."

Then I remembered what Estela told me. "But hey . . . congratulations on winning your solo! That's awesome!"

"Thanks, Cassie," Domingo said. "I wish you had gotten your solo too. It would have been more fun if we both had one." He smiled at me. He reached for my hand and squeezed.

I felt a surge of happiness. Maybe Domingo *did* like me! It was funny, though. Last week, I would have given anything for Domingo to like me as a girlfriend. But last week I wasn't thinking about singing in L.A. Now I didn't know what to think. Domingo was still . . . Domingo. And I still felt butterflies when I looked at him. But . . .

My cell phone interrupted my thoughts. It was Hal. "Hello?" I said. Why would Hal be calling me now?

"Hey, beautiful," he said. "I just heard from L.A. They love the video! But they don't want to wait till tomorrow for pictures. Can you text me a couple of shots tonight? Just something to send on to the music studios?"

"I guess so," I said. "What kind of pictures?"

"Oh, you know," he said. "Like the ones in my office. Some head shots. Some full body. Make them fun." His voice dropped. "Make them hot!"

I felt that shivery feeling again.

"Who was that?" Domingo asked when I hung up.

"Oh, nobody," I said. How lame could I be? "Nobody you know," I added. Like that helped any.

My cell dinged. It was Hal again, texting: How soon can U send the pics, sexy girl?

As soon as I get home from work. I felt strange and daring.

I must have been smiling, because Domingo said, "Well, that sure cheered you up. Good news?"

"Uh . . . no," I said. "Well, I mean, yes . . . sort of. I don't have to work late tonight, that's all." *Stupid, stupid, stupid.*

Domingo brightened. "Why don't I pick you up after your shift?" he asked. "You could come over for a while. Or we could go out for ice cream or something."

"No!" I said too quickly. "My dad's picking me up. I need to go right home. I have a ton of stuff to do: homework . . . and other stuff . . . a ton of other stuff." I couldn't seem to stop babbling.

Domingo's face fell. His hands gripped the steering wheel. "It's okay, Cassie," he said stiffly. "If you don't want to go out with me, just say so. You don't have to make up excuses."

"It isn't that," I started to say. Then I stopped. It was that, sort of. I mean, I did want to go out with Domingo—just not tonight.

Tonight I had to take pictures for Hal. He thought I was special. More than that, he said I wasn't just any client. Hal wanted to make me a star.

How could I get involved with Domingo when my life was going in a whole new direction?

CHAPTER 11

Domingo and I didn't talk much more on the ride to Taco Shack.

"Thanks," I said when we pulled into the parking lot. "See you at school tomorrow!" Then I hurried in to work.

I was lucky. Kelsey traded shifts so I could go home early.

Roz shrugged when I told her. "I don't care if you don't want to work," she said. "As long as you get someone to cover for you.

We need somebody behind the counter at all times."

I called Estela when Roz wasn't looking. "Can you pick me up after work?" I hissed. "It's an emergency!"

"Sure," Estela said. "What's going on? You okay?"

"Just be here at eight!" I said. "I'll tell you then!"

I needed Estela's help. I couldn't take Hal's pictures by myself. But I couldn't let Estela know what was really going on. It was still too early for that. I had my story all ready when she picked me up.

"This has been the worst day!" I said, as I got into Estela's car. "I don't know what happened at glee club! I just fell apart! And then Julia was so good . . ." I didn't have to pretend to sound upset.

Estela looked sympathetic. "It was pretty awful," she agreed. "I felt terrible for you!"

I wished I could tell Estela everything. Tomorrow, I promised myself. This time tomorrow, I wouldn't have any more secrets.

But in the meantime . . .

"I really don't want to be by myself tonight," I told Estela. "Can you come over for a while? Hang out?"

"Sure," she said. "I thought you might say that." Estela motioned to a couple of notebooks in her backseat. "See? I even brought my homework."

"Perfect."

I had a bad moment when we pulled up to my house. Domingo was taking out the garbage. He watched us get out of the car. I tried not to make eye contact.

"Hi, Domingo," Estela called. She nudged me. "Let's invite him over, too!"

"No!" I hurried her into the house. I didn't want to see Domingo's face. My own face burned. Why had I told Domingo that my dad was picking me up after work? Why hadn't I just said Estela was coming over? Now Domingo knew I had lied . . . again.

"Let's just have a girls' night," I told Estela. "I don't feel like hanging out with anyone but you right now."

First we got a snack. Cookie-dough ice cream is always my first choice when I'm upset. We talked a little bit. We listened to music. We even did some homework. Well, for a minute or two. Then I got down to my real business.

"Hey," I said. I tossed down my math book. "I can't concentrate. I just can't stop thinking about sectionals. I'm so mad at myself! I don't know how I can show my face at practice again."

Estela closed her book, too. "I know," she said. "What should we do instead? Want a beauty makeover?"

Estela is so perfect! "Maybe," I said. "Or . . . I know! Help me decide what to wear for sectionals. Even if I don't have a solo, I can look better than Julia!"

Estela brightened. She loves picking out clothes. "Sure!" she said, throwing open my closet door. Estela knows what's in my closet as well as I do. She pulled out a couple of hangers.

"How about black leggings and green halter tunic?" she suggested. "With your amber necklace, you can play up your hair *and* your eyes."

I tried on the chunky amber jewelry. "Here," I said, giving Estela my cell phone. "Do me a favor? Take a picture. I want to try on a bunch of stuff. Then I can compare looks."

I put my hands on my hips and struck a dramatic pose. "How's this?"

Estela grinned. "Hot!" she said. "But shake out your hair. And turn sideways a little. Show Julia your stuff!"

The night turned out to be a lot of fun. Estela played photographer while I tried on practically everything I owned: slinky tank tops, lacy camisoles, long skinny jeans and short, short skirts. Estela gave me advice on each outfit.

I put on my favorite little black dress. It's super short and strapless. It fits like a second skin.

"Wear the plain headband," Estela directed. "And no jewelry! No shoes, either. All right, perfect. Sit on the edge of your bed. Now imagine that you've just come from a party. You're about to slip out of your dress."

Now Estela was really acting her part. "Work with me! Look sexy! You aren't wearing underwear! Domingo's knocking at your bedroom door!"

"Too far!"

We both rolled on the bed laughing.

"Wait!" said Estela, jumping up. "Hold that pose. No, no . . . hug your pillow. Let's see some bedroom eyes!"

Then we really couldn't stop laughing. "Shhhh," I said between gasps. I threw the pillow at Estela. "You'll wake Jake and Ray."

But I really didn't care. It felt so good to be laughing. It seemed like forever since I had been silly with my best friend. I almost forgot why I was taking the pictures.

I remembered after Estela went home. Hal texted me: Where r the pics?

I hesitated only a minute. Then I sent the sexiest pictures to Hal.

Wow! Hot Hot HOT! he texted back.

Somehow, it sounded better when Estela said it.

CHAPTER 12

The next morning was a rush. I had to pack for my photo shoot. I stuffed all my favorite outfits in my backpack. It was a tight fit. I had to leave my math book at home.

"I won't be home till late," I told Mom and Dad. "I'm going straight to work after school." Lying was beginning to seem almost normal.

"Do you need a ride?" Dad asked. "I'm off early today."

I shook my head. "I'm covered," I said. I didn't say who was giving me the ride. So that didn't count as a lie, did it?

"You're never home anymore," said Ray. "It's no fair."

I dropped a kiss on his head. "After today, I'll have more time," I said. "Promise!"

The school day went by in a blur. I left the building as soon as classes ended. I didn't bother going to the music room. Ms. Cao would just lecture me.

"Cassie, baby!" Hal said, when I got in the car. "Great pictures last night! They're just what I wanted. Of course, the resolution wasn't perfect. But we'll fix that today!" He squeezed my knee. Then he moved his hand up my thigh.

I shifted. Hal stroked my leg. He gave one last squeeze. Then he put his hand back on the steering wheel. I felt like a dumb kid again. Hal was an L.A. talent agent, after all. This was just his way of being friendly.

When we got to the hotel room, Hal went over to the little bar. This time, he popped open a bottle of champagne and poured two glasses. "To you, Cassie!" he said, handing me a glass.

I hesitated. I'm not a big drinker. I don't really like the taste of alcohol. And after the horrible way Amber, a girl from school, had died when she drank too much at a party, I've been especially careful.

Hal squeezed my shoulder. "What's wrong, Cassie?" he asked. "You seem a little tense— not like the girl in those photos!"

I decided Hal was right. I *was* a little tense. I took a sip. I had never had champagne before. It tasted good—sweet and bubbly. I took a bigger sip. Stars drink champagne, right? I could feel myself relaxing.

Hal watched me unpack my clothes. "You can change in the bathroom," he said. He fingered my little black dress. "I'm glad you brought this one!"

Then we got to work. Hal told me how to sit and stand. He directed me even more than Estela had. He adjusted my clothes every time I changed outfits.

"Hold your hair on top of your head," he directed. "Smile big. Twirl!" His camera clicked furiously.

"Slide the sweater off your shoulders so just your tank top shows," he said for the next outfit. "Drop the straps on your tank. Lower!" He clicked the camera so fast that I didn't have time to think.

"Unbutton the top button on your jeans," he commanded after I had changed again. "Lean back on the chair. Spread your legs . . . perfect! Hold it!"

Hal handed me my hairbrush. "Bend forward and brush out your hair. Now toss your head back—shake it out and let your hair fall naturally. Great! Perfect! One more . . . hold it! Now lose the tee."

Lose the tee? That would just leave my bra! Hal looked at me over the top of his camera. "Come on, Cassie!" he said. "You run in a sports bra, don't you? Go swimming in a bikini? Why is a bra so different? My agency's going to want to see your figure!"

I hesitated. I couldn't think of an answer, so I pulled my T-shirt over my head. "Good!" said Hal. He clicked away. "Hands behind your head! Look over your left shoulder. Perfect!"

Hal brought the camera up close. "Cross your arms in front," he commanded. "Lean forward . . . more!" *Click.* He snapped a close-up.

It was all happening so fast.

"Straddle the chair," Hal directed. *Click, click.* "Stand up and turn away from me." *Click.* "Hands on your knees. Bend over!" *Click, click, click.*

Hal tossed me my black dress. "Now this one," he said. "Quick!"

I started to go into the bathroom. "Oh, just put it on in here," he said impatiently. "Come on, Cassie! Move it!"

I hopped out of my jeans. I slid the black dress over my head. Hal was right there to zip me up.

"On the bed," he said. "Like you did last night." *Click, click.* He tossed me a pillow. "Roll over! Hug it! Play with it!" He kneeled on the bed over me. *Click, click, click!*

"Good girl!" Hal said. He was breathing hard. He dropped the camera. "I don't think we need this anymore."

And before I knew it, he had unzipped my dress and yanked it over my head. Then he undid my bra and tossed it aside.

"What are you doing?" I said, shocked.

"What does it look like I'm doing?" He pushed me onto my back. "Work's over . . . it's time for fun!"

Hal was strong. He held me down on the bed. His hands were all over me.

"Stop it!" I shouted. "Stop it right now!"

"No stopping now," he murmured, kissing me. He started to unzip his pants.

I didn't even think. I jerked my knee up, hard. I screamed, loud.

Hal cursed. He slapped me across the face. I rolled off the bed and grabbed my jeans.

"You little—," Hal cursed again. "What the hell do you think you're doing?"

"I'm leaving!" I said, putting on my jeans. I was shaking. "I never said you could do this!"

"You didn't have to say it, Cassie! You showed me exactly what you wanted!"

"I wanted you to take me to L.A.!" I cried. "You said you'd make me a star! You said I was special!"

Hal gave a short laugh. "Special! Girls like you are a dime a dozen, Cassie!"

I felt like I had been slapped again. "No! They aren't!" Now I really was crying. "I want my money back! And my pictures!"

"You want your money back!" Hal jeered. "And your pictures! Oh, that's a riot." He came toward me. I grabbed my T-shirt and purse and backed away.

Hal had an ugly look on his face. His eyes were hard and glittering. "You can have your money back, Cassie," he said harshly, "and your pictures." He grabbed me by the wrist. "Just take off those pants, and let's finish what we started!"

I pulled away. "Let me go!" I cried, running to the door. "I'm telling my parents!"

Hal laughed. "Tell them what? That you came up to my hotel room of your own free will—twice—that you sexted me pictures from your bedroom, that you stripped and asked me to take pictures of you today? Remember . . . I have your pictures. If you leave now, I'll use them however I want!"

I wrenched open the door and fled. Hal's laugh followed me like a bad dream as I struggled into my T-shirt and ran down the hotel hallway.

CHAPTER 13

I was shaking like crazy when I left the hotel. I ran blindly for a few blocks. I didn't care where I was going. I just wanted to get away from that hotel.

Then I slowed down. It was almost dusk. Rain was falling, making things seem darker. I looked around. Where was I?

I couldn't stop shivering. I was cold and wet . . . and scared. I couldn't believe what had happened back at the hotel. Hal had seemed so nice before!

Thinking about Hal made me even more frightened. What if he came after me? What if he found me out here, alone?

I fumbled in my purse. Yes! My cell phone was still there. I didn't even stop to think. Shakily, I scrolled through my contacts and found Domingo's number.

"Can you pick me up?" I blurted as soon as he answered. "Right now?"

"Cassie?" Domingo said. "Where are you? What's wrong?"

I was crying so hard, I could barely talk. "I don't know! Somewhere . . . I don't know! Please . . . just come get me!"

"I'm on my way, Cassie," he said. "Just tell me where you are. Are you at Taco Shack?"

"No! Downtown! I'm downtown!" I looked around for a street sign, and told him where I was. "Please hurry!" Then I totally panicked. "Don't hang up! Please, please, don't hang up on me!"

Domingo talked to me the whole time he drove. By the time his car squealed to a stop in front of me, my cell was nearly dead and I had almost stopped crying.

"Cassie!" he said as he jumped out of the car. "What happened?" He got me into the front seat. He put his jacket around my shoulders. "It's all right," he kept saying. "You're all right now."

I was so relieved to see him, I started crying all over again. "It was so awful," I sobbed. "It was the worst thing ever!" And without really meaning to, I blurted out the whole horrible story.

Domingo looked furious when I finished. He cursed under his breath. "That..." He spun the steering wheel around. "I'm going back to that hotel right now," he said grimly. I'm not joking. "That guy's going to get seriously messed up!"

"No!" I was terrified all over again. "Please, no! I don't want to go back there! I just want to go home! Please, Domingo!"

Domingo looked at me for a long minute. I could tell he was still furious. "Okay," he said finally. "Okay, Cassie. I'll take you home first.

You need to tell your parents what happened. But after I drop you off, I'm going back to that hotel. That guy isn't going to get away with this!"

Tell my parents! I could never tell my parents what I had done. I was already sorry I had told Domingo. Now that I wasn't so scared, I was just embarrassed—totally embarrassed and humiliated. Hal had my pictures—those horrible, terrible pictures. If I told my parents, I was sure he'd spread those pictures everywhere. How could I have been so stupid?

"Just take me home," I begged Domingo. "I'm okay now. I'm not hurt. It's all over . . . there's no reason to tell my parents. And you don't need to go back to the hotel. Really! I was stupid, and I made a dumb mistake! But it's over now! It isn't a big deal!"

Domingo looked at me again. "You *are* stupid," he said flatly, "if you think this was just some dumb little mistake and that it's over now. That guy hit you and nearly raped you. He could have killed you! This *is* a big deal,

Cassie . . . a really big deal. And if you won't tell your parents, I will!"

Domingo turned the car around again. He headed straight for my house.

Once again, Domingo and I finished a car ride in complete and total silence.

CHAPTER 14

Domingo pulled into his driveway and switched off the engine. We sat there for a minute. I knew I had to say something.

"Domingo?" I took a deep breath. I was suddenly exhausted. "You're right. I . . . I have to tell my parents what happened tonight. Even though I got myself into a mess, I can't get out of it alone."

I didn't want to cry again. "Thank you for coming to get me," I said in a low voice. "I'm

85

sorry I had to call you. I'm sorry for lying. I wish I could undo everything. I wish . . ." I stopped. What else was there to say?

Domingo got out of the car and opened my door for me. "Come on," he said. We walked up the sidewalk. When we got to my front door, Domingo stopped.

"I'm not sorry you called me," he said. That was all. But it was enough.

I'm glad Domingo was with me when I told my parents. Mom and Dad are usually pretty calm about things. They don't blow up like a lot of parents. But this was different. My dad especially went nuts. He wanted to go straight back to the hotel and clobber Hal. My mom wouldn't let him.

"Stop it," she snapped. "I don't need a daughter *and* a husband in trouble tonight. I'm calling the police to handle this." She held an ice pack to my face with one hand. She reached for the phone with the other.

"No!" I burst out. "I don't want the police!" The thought of telling a strange police officer about tonight made me feel sick.

"It isn't about what you want anymore," Mom said sharply. "Doing what you want nearly got you raped! You could have been killed!" Now she was the one who burst into tears.

That's when Domingo spoke up. "What about Selena?" he asked. "You could call Selena."

I think we all breathed a sigh of relief. Selena is Domingo's older sister. She's a police detective. I've known Selena all my life. I could talk to Selena.

Selena came right over. She took one look at me and called the station. She gave them Hal's room number at the Dahlia Hotel. "A squad car is on its way," she told us.

Then Selena sent Domingo home. He didn't want to leave me. "Later, brother," Selena said firmly. "I need to talk to Cassie alone."

Selena made me tell her every single thing about my meetings with Hal. She went over my story again and again. She asked me questions and wrote down all my answers. She looked at the red mark on my face where Hal slapped me.

"I'm going to take you to the hospital," she said. "You need to be examined by a doctor. And then I want you to sign a statement."

"Do I have to?" I begged. "I just want to go to bed!"

My dad put his arm around me. "Can she do this tomorrow?" he asked. "You know the guy's name. You know what hotel room he's in. Shouldn't you be arresting him instead of badgering Cassie?"

"Look," Selena said patiently. "I know this is hard. But I think I know this guy. If he's who I think he is, Cassie isn't the first girl he has attacked. I have a file on him a mile thick. He—"

Selena's cell buzzed. She answered and listened for a few minutes. "Yeah, that's what I thought," she said to the person on the other end. She gave a few instructions. Then she snapped her phone shut.

"He's skipped out of the hotel," she said. "The room's been cleaned out. He probably threw Cassie's clothes and backpack in some dumpster. We'll check the area, but we may never find anything."

"But you know his name," Mom said. "You have the business card he gave Cassie!"

Selena shook her head. "It's fake. He checked into the hotel using a different name. That's probably fake, too. Without a license plate, I can't put out a bulletin on his car. He has probably already ditched his cell phone." Selena looked angry. "He's very good at preying on vulnerable kids."

I still didn't understand. "But what about the agency in L.A.? Can't you call STAR 1?"

Selena sat down on the couch next to me. "There is no agency in L.A.," she said bluntly. "Hal's a crook. He told you a bunch of lies so that he could take advantage of you. He wanted sex, and he wanted your money. That's all."

I felt sick to my stomach. "He told me that I was special," I whispered.

"He told a lot of other girls that they were special, too," Selena said sharply. "Listen to me, Cassie. I know you've had a rotten night. But this guy's scum. Come to the hospital with me. Let a doctor examine you. Sign a statement. Help me stop this guy before he hurts another girl."

And in the end, that's what I did. I was glad Selena was with me. I knew she was trying to make it as easy as she could.

But it was still the worst night of my life.

CHAPTER 15

I didn't go to school the next day. I spent most of the day sleeping—and having really hard conversations with my parents.

"How could you do it, Cassie?" Dad asked. He looked tired and sad. "The hotel room, I mean. And those pictures . . ."

"I don't know," I said miserably. "Taking the pictures with Estela was fun. We were just goofing around. At the hotel . . ." My voice trailed off. I tried to answer honestly.

"At first it was exciting. And then . . . it all just happened so fast. I guess I wasn't thinking, really . . ."

I remembered what Selena had told us last night.

"He has the pictures," she had said. "The ones you texted him and the ones he took. What he does with them is anybody's guess. If he posts or publishes them, maybe we can trace him . . . but maybe not." Selena shrugged. "You're just going to have to live with this, Cassie. Those pictures could show up any time, any place. Some mistakes don't have easy fixes."

Mom was still picking at my story, like Ray or Jake picking at a scab. "And all those lies, Cassie . . . about glee club and work, about Jake being sick—how could you?" she asked.

"I don't know," I kept repeating. "I just don't know! First I wanted to surprise everyone with the *America's Next Star* tryout. Then I wanted to surprise everyone with L.A. I thought it would be cool. He said . . ."

I couldn't make myself say Hal's name. I shuddered just thinking about him.

Mom and Dad were quiet. Then Mom took my chin in her hand. "You are special, Cassie," she said softly. "To all of us who know you. And someday, maybe you really will go to L.A. But it will be on your own honest terms."

"In the meantime," added Dad. "You just keep on doing what you do best. Go to school. Sing in glee club. Be a good daughter and sister and friend. Try to put this behind you."

Dad still looked sad. We all knew that putting this behind me wasn't going to be easy.

Ray and Jake were really nice to me when they got home from school. They had slept through everything last night. They didn't know anything about what had happened. They just thought I was home sick.

"Do you want a Popsicle?" Jake asked. "That's what I like when I'm sick."

"Or Jell-O," Ray said. "We could make you cherry Jell-O."

I wanted to cry, they were so sweet. I thought about those pictures again. What if my little brothers clicked on a computer some day and saw them? How could I ever explain? Living with this was going to be harder than I thought.

The next day, Domingo gave me a ride to school. He held my hand and walked me to my locker—sort of like I was a little kid who needed protecting. But also sort of like I was his girlfriend.

Estela was waiting at our locker. She glared at me. Then she and Domingo exchanged glances. Clearly, they had talked.

"Estela," I started. Then I stopped. From now on, I had to be completely honest. "I don't know what I can say."

Estela didn't let me finish. "I know exactly what you can say," she said. "You can say, 'Estela, I'm sorry. You're my best friend and I lied to you. I betrayed your trust. I hurt your feelings. I didn't even call you when I was in trouble and needed help.'"

"Estela," I repeated. "I'm sorry. You're my best friend and I lied to you. I betrayed your trust. I hurt your feelings. I didn't even call you when I was in trouble and needed help."

Estela held up her hand. "Don't interrupt," she said. She didn't look quite so mad. "I'm not done. I practiced this."

I almost smiled.

"Then you can say, 'Estela, I failed as a friend. But I promise to be better. And if any scumbag creep ever bothers me again, I'll call my best friend Estela to break his legs.'"

I burst into tears—right there in the school hallway.

Estela hugged me. "Oh, Cassie! First I was so mad at you. Then I was so worried about you! Are you okay?"

I told her everything then. "And he has all my pictures!" I wailed.

Estela shrugged. "That sucks," she said. "But I've seen worse on the Internet. And I'd rather have a few embarrassing pictures floating around than be raped. You were lucky, Cassie. Stupid . . . but lucky."

We were going to be late for math. We walked down the hall. I imagined kids were looking at me and whispering.

"Does everyone know?" I asked.

Estela tossed her head. "Not from me and Domingo, they don't."

"Selena's talking to Mrs. Nuñez," I said. "I guess I have to see a counselor, too." I wondered if this would ever really go away.

The next hard thing came in glee club. Domingo and Estela walked into the music room with me. They nodded encouragingly as I went up to Ms. Cao.

I took a deep breath. "Ms. Cao?" I said. "I'm sorry I skipped yesterday . . . and the day before . . . and all the other times. I . . . I've been going through a bad time. But that's no excuse. I shouldn't have let the club down." I couldn't think of anything else to say. "I'm sorry."

Ms. Cao studied me. "Mrs. Nuñez called me into her office this morning," she said. "She told me a little bit about what happened.

96

She thought I might have heard of other kids getting in trouble like you."

Ms. Cao sighed. "Oh, Cassie. I'm so sorry for all this. What can I say? I can't give you back the solo for sectionals. Julia earned it, fair and square. But you're just a junior. There will be other solos. And you'll still be in our group numbers."

"You mean I can go to sectionals?" I asked. "Even after all my skips?"

Ms. Cao nodded. "Under the circumstances, yes. And one more thing: I want you to come by my office after practice. I have an application for a summer internship you might like. It's for the community musical theater that I direct. It's a lot of work and not much pay. A summer musical isn't L.A. But it's good experience. Now . . . find your place. We need to get started!"

I took my spot on the risers. Ms. Cao sat at the piano and started our warm-up exercises. My first few notes were shaky. I had been away from glee club too long.

But my voice got stronger with each note. Estela and Domingo smiled their support.

By the time we finished warm-ups, I was feeling the music. I was finding my rhythm. The whole horrible experience with Hal was fading.

I was beginning to feel like myself again. I was singing with my whole heart. And that was special enough for now.

About the Author

Charnan Simon lives in Seattle, Washington, and has written more than one hundred books for young readers. Her two daughters are now mostly grown up, and she misses having teenagers running in and out of the house.

SOUTHSIDE HIGH

ARE YOU A SURVIVOR?

check out all the books in the

SURVIVING SOUTH SIDE

collection.

Bad Deal

Fish hates having to take ADHD meds. They help him concentrate but also make him feel weird. So when a cute girl needs a boost to study for tests, Fish offers her one of his pills. Soon more kids want pills, and Fish likes the profits. To keep from running out, Fish finds a doctor who sells phony prescriptions. But suddenly the doctor is arrested. Fish realizes he needs to tell the truth. But will that cost him his friends?

Recruited

Kadeem is a star quarterback for Southside High. He is thrilled when college scouts seek him out. One recruiter even introduces him to a college cheerleader and gives him money to have a good time. But then officials start to investigate illegal recruiting. Will Kadeem decide to help their investigation, even though it means the end of the good times? What will it do to his chances of playing in college?

Benito Runs

Benito's father had been in Iraq for over a year. When he returns, Benito's family life is not the same. Dad suffers from PTSD—post-traumatic stress disorder—and yells constantly. Benito can't handle seeing his dad so crazy, so he decides to run away. Will Benny find a new life? Or will he learn how to deal with his dad—through good times and bad?

PLAN B

Lucy has her life planned: she'll graduate and join her boyfriend at college in Austin. She'll become a Spanish teacher and of course they'll get married. So there's no reason to wait, right? They try to be careful, but Lucy gets pregnant. Lucy's plan is gone. How will she make the most difficult decision of her life?

BEATEN

Keah's a cheerleader and Ty's a football star, so they seem like the perfect couple. But when they have their first fight, Ty is beginning to scare Keah with his anger. Then after losing a game, Ty goes ballistic and hits Keah repeatedly. Ty is arrested for assault, but Keah still secretly meets up with Ty. How can Keah be with someone she's afraid of? What's worse—flinching every time your boyfriend gets angry, or being alone?

Shattered Star

Cassie is the best singer at Southside and dreams of being famous. She skips school to try out for a national talent competition. But her hopes sink when she sees the line. Then a talent agent shows up, and Cassie is flattered to hear she has "the look" he wants. Soon she is lying and missing rehearsal to meet with him. And he's asking her for more each time. How far will Cassie go for her shot at fame?

THE PROTECTORS

Luke's life has never been "normal." How could it be, with
his mother holding séances and his stepfather working as a
mortician? But living in a funeral home never bothered Luke
until the night of his mom's accident.

Sounds of screaming now shatter Luke's dreams. And his
stepfather is acting even stranger. When bodies in the funeral
home start delivering messages, Luke is certain that he's nuts. As
he tries to solve his mother's death, Luke discovers a secret more
horrifying than any nightmare.

SKIN

It looks like a pizza exploded on Nick Barry's face. But bad skin
is the least of his problems. His bones feel like living ice. A
strange rash—like scratches—seems to be some sort of ancient
code. And then there's the anger ...

Something evil is living under Nick's skin. Where did it
come from? What does it want? With the help of a dead kid's
diary, a nun, and a local professor, Nick slowly finds out what's
wrong with him. But there's still one question that Nick must
face alone: how do you destroy an evil that's *inside* you?

THAW

A July storm caused a major power outage in Bridgewater. Now a research project at the Institute for Cryogenic Experimentation has been ruined, and the thawed-out bodies of twenty-seven federal inmates are missing.

At first, Dani didn't think much of the news. But after her best friend Jake disappears, a mysterious visitor connects the dots for Dani. Jake has been taken in by a cult. To get him back, Dani must enter a dangerous, alternate reality where a defrosted cult leader is beginning to act like some kind of god.

UNTHINKABLE

Omar Phillips is Bridgewater High's favorite teen author. His fans can't wait for his next horror story. But lately Omar's imagination has turned against him. Horrifying visions of death and destruction haunt him. The only way to stop the visions is to write them down. Until they start coming true . . .

Enter Sophie Minax, the mysterious girl who's been following Omar at school. "I'm one of you," Sophie says. She tells Omar how to end the visions—but the only thing worse than Sophie's cure may be what happens if he ignores it.

THE CLUB

The club started innocently enough. Bored after school, Josh and his friends decided to try out an old board game. Called "Black Magic," it promised players good fortune at the expense of those who have wronged them.

But when the club members' luck starts skyrocketing—and horror befalls their enemies—the game stops being a joke. How can they stop what they've unleashed? Answers lie in an old diary—but ending the game may be deadlier than any curse.

MESSAGES FROM BEYOND

Some guy named Ethan has been texting Cassie. He seems to know all about her—but she can't place him. He's not in the yearbook either. Cassie thinks one of her friends is punking her. But she can't ignore the strange coincidences—like how Ethan looks just like the guy in her nightmares.

Cassie's search for Ethan leads her to a shocking discovery—and a struggle for her life. Will Cassie be able to break free from her mysterious stalker?